JUST MY LOST TREASURE

BY MERCER MAYER

For Sidney,
a sweetie pie!

HARPER FESTIVAL
An Imprint of HarperCollinsPublishers

Manufactured in China.
For information address HarperCollins Children's Books, a division of HarperCollins Publishers, 195 Broadway, New York, NY 10007.
Library of Congress catalog card number: 2013956395
ISBN 978-0-06-147806-2
18 19 20   SCP   10 9 8 7 6   ❖   First Edition

 A Big Tuna Trading Company, LLC/J.R. Sansevere Book
www.harpercollinschildrens.com   www.littlecritter.com

"Little Critter," Mom called, "please come to the laundry room."
"Oh no," I thought, "what did I do now?"
I don't think I left bubble gum in my pockets.

"You are missing one sock from each pair!" said Mom.
"They just disappeared," I said.
"Find where they disappeared to," Mom said.

I looked in my closet.
No socks . . . but I found my lost
Space Ranger rocket ship.

I looked under my bed. No socks . . . but I found my
Super Space robot. It had been missing forever.

I went to look in my little sister's room,
but she wouldn't let me in.

"Maybe a sock is in the sandbox," I thought.
I took my shovel outside to dig.

I dug and dug. No sock . . .
but I found my Billy Bear bulldozer.
What a lucky day!

Mom said I had to keep looking. I called Gator.
"Gator, did I leave any socks at your house?" I asked.
"I don't know," Gator said. "Come over and look."

I went to Gator's house. No socks . . .
but we found a bug and a green snake.

I found my Critter Scout bugle in the garden.
I was finding lost treasure everywhere!

Then I went to Tiger's house.
"Have I left any socks here?" I asked.
We checked in Tiger's laundry room,
but his mom made us go outside.

"Let's look in my clubhouse
above the garage," Tiger said.
No socks . . . but we found my
bomber jacket and my cowboy hat.

I passed Timothy's house on the way home.
I rang the doorbell. Timothy's mother answered.
"Hello, Little Critter," she said.

"Did I leave any socks here?" I asked.
"No, but I have something else you left here," she said.
She handed me my giant stuffed gorilla that talks.
I had no idea I had so many lost toys!

I thought I'd go by the park before I went home.
A little raccoon kid was playing basketball with his dad.
I watched them for a minute.

"That's mine," I said when I saw the ball.

"My name is on the side."

His dad looked. There was my name.

I was so happy, but the little raccoon wasn't.

I let him borrow my ball.
I couldn't carry much else.
And I found even more stuff in the weeds.

It was my Red Racer wagon.
Now I could carry all of my treasure home.
I also found my hockey stick,
my Sluggo Duggo bat, and my lasso.

I found my Super XL keyboard at Henrietta's house.

I went home with no socks but lots of treasure.

Mom heard me and called, "Little Critter, is that you?"
"Yes, Mom," I answered.
"Look what I found," she said.

Mom was cleaning out Blue's bed.
There were all the missing socks!

I showed Mom all my lost treasure.
"Mom, you found the socks," I said,
"and I found my lost treasure."

"Blue buried your socks just like his lost treasure," Mom said. "Now I can wash socks, and you can put your toys back where they belong."

"They aren't just toys, Mom," I said.
"They're just my lost treasure."